Goldiella

The story of a just right girl with a
happily ever after dream.

By

Tonia Christine Halley

Cover illustration by Noah William Rogers

Preface

This is a story from the life of a family living a life with a loved one with autism. Yet, this is not just a story about living with a family member with autism. It is about how something good, and even amazing can come despite something so hard, mind boggling, and even painful. Autism is more well- known now that it ever has been. We have seen many autistic people show amazing talent and skill and overcome obstacles that seem almost impossible. This is the story of how through our great and amazing God, the impossible things become possible. It is to Him that we give the glory for all those impossible things. May anyone who reads this book, be encouraged in their own impossible trials and find true amazement in God alone.

Chapters

Chapter 1 Once Upon a time, Goldi.......

For you formed my inward parts; you knitted me together in my mother's womb.

Psalm 139:13

Once upon a time, in the cold of winter, a doctor announced: "Expect a baby in August!" Mrs. Howard was immediately warmed all over. She repeated the announcement to her husband who immediately began to call his wife *momma* and himself *papa*. There were signs that followed making the news more and more certain. Mrs. Howard's tummy had swelled up like a pumpkin. She felt the baby kick one night, while listening to the violin solo at the symphony. The surest sign of all, was when they saw the baby with their own eyes, curled up, sucking its thumb on the ultrasound screen, and they heard the light and airy heartbeat like a gentle breeze announcing: "I'm coming soon!" After nine months of anticipation, their baby girl's big blue eyes met the wide world.

"Her name is Marigold Ellanora Howard," announced her mother. Some popular names sounded a bit like a puppy or one of the Radio City Music Hall Rockettes. Both parents had both thought very carefully about the perfect name. They imagined calling their child in for dinner. They thought about the name the teacher would say when taking attendance at school. They thought how it would sound on graduation day when announced over the microphone. Most of all, they considered the moment when their child would introduce themselves to another, and then that name might mean *friend*. The Howards decided upon *Marigold* after the flower that shines brightly for a long summer. Her middle name was *Ellanora*, after her dear great grandmother.

"What a beautiful name!" said the nurse after she had printed it on the baby's birth certificate.

"She IS beautiful!" said her mother seeing her daughter for the first time.

"She has golden locks, just like another girl I know," said Mr. Howard seeing the tiny yellow hairs on her baby bald head.

As Marigold grew, several discoveries told them that she was quite like that girl in the fairy tale. When Mrs. Howard read that the vacuum was like the sound in the womb, she figured she could clean the rugs while Marigold napped. But this little trick led to loud screaming warning her that the vacuum was excruciatingly "too noisy". In order for Mrs. Howard to get her work done, it was only just right if Marigold wore headphones. When Mr. Howard took the car to the car wash and Goldi rode along resting peacefully in the back seat, until the brushes spun and the water squirted, and she practically burst out of her safety straps. Her clothes were only worn comfortably when all the tags were cut off, her meals consisted of only crunchy and crispy foods, and the continuous sound of *"Rock-a-bye Baby"* playing softly at night, made for the sweetest of dreams.

The Howards became accustomed to their daughter's quirks and didn't worry much about them. They simply thought they she would grow out of them in time.

But the waiting only brought more mystery. Mrs. Howard had been folding laundry when she heard a loud thud followed by some loud screaming. There she found Marigold lying face down on the floor at the bottom of the stairs.

"Dear, dear," she said holding her daughter tightly. "Did you fall down the stairs?"

Marigold pushed Mrs. Howard away. Her mother reached for her again, but Marigold resisted once more. She merely sat there crying not accepting any comfort. Poor Mrs. Howard felt hopelessly discouraged. The only comfort Marigold would tolerate is a gentle back rubbing.

"Maybe she was too scared at the moment," suggested Mr. Howard.

"Not accept a hug from her own mother? That's just dreadful!" said Mrs. Howard.

Marigold cried again when she bumped her head on the kitchen wall. This time, Mrs. Howard offered Marigold a beautiful doll with golden hair just like hers. It had a pink dress with tiny roses embroidered at the hem. Mrs. Howard hoped Marigold would pick it up, hold it, and maybe even put it to sleep. Marigold threw the doll down on the floor and just continued to cry. Mrs. Howard rubbed her back and rubbed her back and then sat the doll in her room in a small rocking chair, hoping she would notice it again and begin to play with it.

Then one evening after dinner, Marigold twirled and danced for them in the living room.

"Isn't that so cute?" said Mr. Howard.

"It's absolutely adorable!" said Mrs. Howard.

"Achee do sitz" she said "Fzitooma litza ramo"!

"She's talking!" exclaimed Mrs. Howard.

"And she is looking right at us! She's even gesturing!" exclaimed Mrs. Howard.

"Kachoo, mumaj!" said Marigold

"She certainly is talking!" stated Mr. Howard, "But what is she saying?"

"I have no idea," said Mrs. Howard.

Marigold continued to say more. They leaned in to hear something they could understand.

"Maybe she knows another language!" said Mr. Howard.

The very next day, Mrs. Howard clung to a notepad. She found Marigold did say something. She said *camera* and *swimming*, along with *yes*, *no*, *daddy*, *mommy*, and *carrot*. At the end of the day, Marigold had said 20 miraculous words.

Two summers later, a small bundle had arrived wrapped in blue blankets, and in a cozy baby seat. She tiptoed over to it, reached out inches away, and barely tapped the top. She backed away quickly when the bundle inside moved. She tried again getting close enough to touch it for she had never seen such a sight before, and it seemed to be staying.

"Marigold, meet your baby brother!" Mr. Howard announced.

"This is Henry!" exclaimed Mrs. Howard.

In her persistence, Marigold had gently kissed the top of her baby brother's head. She kissed him there every morning, and his eyes lit up.

When they both were hobbling on two feet, they did what young siblings close in age do. They licked popsicles on the swing set. They rode their tricycles all around the driveway and chased each other around the kitchen table after dinner.

One day, when Marigold and Henry were wrestling on the living room floor for the same ball that lit up when it bounced, a curious thing happened.

"Ball!" Henry said, "Ball!" he said again loud and clear.

"He's talking!" Mrs. Howard exclaimed.

"Cgtrl!" said Marigold twirling and twirling. After twirling, she said more:

"Ahz ochee an oyn theletem!"

"Is she?" asked Mr. Howard.

Mrs. Howard hugged Henry and gave him the ball. Then they both applauded Marigold's speech as they often did and puzzled harder over the obvious fact that Henry was talking but Marigold really wasn't.

Henry was soon a walking encyclopedia at two years of age. His parents were so very proud. Marigold continued to be eloquent in some mysterious language. Her parents continued to be confused.

"We just can't go on trying to guess what she's saying!" cried Mr. Howard, "We can't wait anymore for something that just might not happen. We have to see a professional."

An appointment was made with an expert. It seemed like they had every piece of information needed about her except for her shoe size. After some weeks, there was a diagnosis.

"Marigold is autistic." the doctor said.

Mrs. Howard teared up. Mr. Howard sighed.

Mrs. Howard had heard that label before. Never once did she think it would one day mean something more than that.

"Tell us more doctor," requested Mr. Howard.

"Goldi's brain is different than the normal child," informed Dr. Peters.

"Starting with the word 'different' can never be a good thing coming from a doctor," said Mrs. Howard.

"How different?" Mr. Howard inquired being interested in details before coming to conclusion.

"Do you have a mixing spoon in your kitchen?" asked Dr. Peters.

"Yes," said Mrs. Howard with raised eyebrows.

"Is it handy?" he continued.

"Well, yes, for stirring." answered Mrs. Howard.

"Do you have an electric mixer?" he asked continuing to prod.

"Yes, we have that too," answered Mr. Howard.

"And what do you do with it?"

"We mix things like cake batter and cookie dough," Mrs. Howard said in a somewhat irritated tone.

"You use both those kitchen tools?" he asked.

Mrs. Howard sighed again. Kitchen talk was the least of her interests at a time like this.

"We do." Mr. Howard answered cooperatively.

"Would you use your mixing spoon to stir cookie dough?"

"No, it doesn't make the batter smooth like the mixer does." Mrs. Howard informed.

"Would you use the mixer to stir your soup?"

"Goodness no! It would splatter all over the place!" exclaimed Mrs. Howard, "Now, could you please tell us what this all has to do with our Goldi?" she asked in frustration.

"You see, Marigold's brain is like a mixing spoon. It can mix things up but might not blend everything together as smoothly. Her mixing spoon brain works harder and often might take more time to do its job. Our brains are more like the mixer. It blends everything together quite smoothly in no time."

"Well then how did she get to be a mixing spoon in the first place?" asked Mrs. Howard.

"That mystery may never be solved. But even so, there are recipes that call for the mixing by hand. Those recipes turn out just right." Dr. Peters concluded.

"Talk plainly to us please. Will Marigold ever live a normal life?" asked Mrs. Howard with a scratch in her tone.

Dr. Peters took off his glasses, rubbed his eyes, and he himself sighed.

"Yes, will she? I mean, how bad is it?" asked Mrs. Howard.

"It does no good to try to find out how bad or why this is. Normal isn't possible. But that's not necessarily a bad thing. There may be something even better than a normal life for Marigold. The sky can still be the limit for what life brings. With autism, there is first, something unique. It's interesting, and sometimes, even mysterious. Marigold is autistic and always will be. You mustn't try to find out why she is this way, but instead discover who she is and how rich your life will be for having her as your daughter."

The Howards sat speechless for a moment. There were feelings of disappointment and fear. The news was so unexpected. Now, they had to somehow make the best of it, not just for themselves, but for Marigold too.

 "I guess since we saw her golden hairs on her head, we knew that she was our own Goldilocks," concluded her mother," and we're in for a real walk in the woods."

"And just like Goldilocks, she's not going to have a normal life, she will have an adventure," added Mr. Howard.

Dr. Peters provided them with a list of therapists and resources. They went home with a file of papers, a book for recommended reading, and a heavy heart.

 First, a speech therapist worked weekly with Marigold to get her really talking. She showed pictures and matched them with words. The Howards practiced "talking" at home. Sometimes at dinner, the Howards would make attempt to have a nice family conversation around the table. Mrs. Howard would begin with questions every parent asked like "What did you do today?" or "Do you like the mashed potatoes?" Marigold would just sit there with wandering eyes. They longed for her to just say something, **anything** that made sense. Something that wasn't said in a foreign language from nowhere. They longed to know that she was there and not caught up in some world they couldn't reach. Marigold was always silent while Henry rambled on and on about HIS day.

Then one night, Mr. Howard read Marigold's favorite bedtime story.

"SOMEONE HAS BEEN SLEEPING IN MY BED!" he read in superb Papa Bear voice.

"Goldi! Goldi is just right!!" Marigold said giggling.

"Yes, that's right my Goldi girl! Just right!" said Mr. Howard kissing her on the forehead.

Goldi snuggled down in the covers and began to dream sweet dreams.

Chapter 2 Into the Woods

In this world, you will have trouble, but take heart, I have overcome the world. John 16:33

A large grove of trees behind the Howard's house provided Henry and Goldi with a special playground. While Henry spied on neighbors from his favorite tree branch, Goldi skipped so much among the trees, that the ground had smoothed over to make a perfect path. There were four large fallen tree branches that Mr. Howard had made into a square. Goldi had filled it with lots of fallen leaves and formed them into three neat piles. There was a tree stump for a table. Goldi had put three large rocks for bowls and gathered three sticks for spoons. While Henry came down from the treetops and was soon playing catch with his friends, Goldi stayed contentedly in the woods - her storybook stage.

"She's been out there for hours," said Mrs. Howard as she looked out the window.

"No doubt she's acting out Goldilocks again," said Mr. Howard.

"It's all she knows," said her mother worriedly. "She should be playing with some other girls her age."

The Howards attempted to help matters by inviting Matilda, their neighbor across the street to play.

"Goldi, say 'hello'," her mother coaxed when she arrived.

Goldi hid behind Mrs. Howard's knees.

Mrs. Howard gently nudged her forward.

Goldi looked far away and then buried her chin in her chest.

"Why don't you take Matilda up to your room?" Mrs. Howard suggested.

Goldi finally ran upstairs, and Matilda followed.

Her room was decorated in pink splashes. There was a small bed covered in a simple flower pattern with some stuffed animals. The room looked like fairy tale land consisting of a dollhouse, a fairy house, a castle, and several little houses. Then Matilda saw the doll in the rocking chair. The one that had sat there since Mrs. Howard tried to get Marigold to notice her and hold her. She had sat there quiet and still since that day.

"She looks just like you," Matilda said picking her up, "What's her name?" asked Matilda

"Dolly," she answered.

"No, I mean what's your doll's **name**?" Matilda insisted.

"Doll," Goldi repeated.

"You haven't named her yet?" Matilda asked.

"Dolly." Goldi said. She grabbed the doll away from Matilda and put her back in the rocking chair.

Matilda shrugged her shoulders.

"She's pretty. Can't we play with her?" she asked.

Goldi didn't answer. She was busy putting little fabric squares for blankets over all the tiny doll figures in each house.

"Time for bed, "she said to each one. "Sleep tight."

"Can't we play with them?" Matilda asked.

"They have to go to sleep," said Goldi.

"But it's daytime." Matilda said, "We could play house with them."

"I have to put them to sleep." Goldi said.

Matilda went to the dollhouse and uncovered one of the dolls.

"What's for breakfast?" she said in a high-pitched voice.

"No! "It's time for them to sleep!" Goldi yelled snatching the doll out of Matilda's hand.

Matilda froze then left the room.

"I'm going home," she told Mrs. Howard.

"Already?" Mrs. Howard said with surprise.

The front door closed with a thud.

Goldi looked at her resting dolls. The quiet opened her eyes to loneliness. She had done what she learned from Miss Suanne, her therapist, when taught how to play:

"First, hold the baby like this," Miss Suzanne had said cradling the doll, *"Then you swing her back and forth in your arms and you sing 'Rock a bye baby ...."*

Goldi held her doll upright and scrunched it up against her chin.

"Rock a bye baby", Goldi whispered.

"Then you cover her up and say "Good night! Sleep tight!" Miss Suzanne said.

"Sleep Tight," whispered Goldi.

As she watched Matilda walk home through her window, she wondered *"What comes after sleep tight?"*

She went out alone to the swing set and made her toes touched the clouds, and the warm breeze kissed her cheeks. Swinging made her feel happy again.

"Only a few more days until kindergarten," Mrs. Howard said worriedly, "I hope she's ready."

"Therapy has helped," said Mr. Howard "Ready or not, here she comes!"

On the first day, Goldi wore her free- flowing cotton dress. Her socks bunched up inside her bright pink tennis shoes. Her wind comb hair flew around mischievously. Around her neck, she wore a necklace from a sensory tool catalog. It had light, smooth, soft beads especially designed for feeling, squeezing, and even chewing away anxieties. Goldi caressed it when she entered the Kindergarten classroom.

"Welcome!" said Miss Violet on one knee, "Would you like to play while we wait for other friends to arrive?"

Goldi scanned the room like a searchlight. It seemed everything a child could want was available for play.

Miss Violet led her to the dollhouse.

"Too busy," said Goldi.

Her teacher shrugged her shoulders and led her to the play kitchen.

"Too messy!" said Goldi.

A crash of building blocks caught Goldi's attention.

"Just right!" Goldi exclaimed as she rushed over and began to stack blocks.

At the crash, Goldi clapped, flapped, and jumped. So, did all the other block builders.

"Things are going to be just fine!" Miss Violet told Mr. and Mrs. Howard.

"How about that?" said Mr. Howard. "One of the bunch!"

In Kindergarten, every student was a mystery. Jerome picked the lint off the story rug at reading time. Annie tugged strands of hair often. Xavier needed reminding to use the restroom at least three times a day. Miss Violet just let it all be and enjoyed teaching her class all the "Firsts".

She gave Goldi markers to glide just right on paper. The snacks were crunchy, play time was full of block building, and the stories she read were like listening to dear friends.

One afternoon, Miss Violet showed the class, a book cover for Goldi's favorite fairy tale. There was the most beautiful forest Goldi had ever seen with bears that looked like Teddy Bears. A girl with golden locks wore a colored pink dress that she was certain hung in her own closet. She began to bounce and flap when Miss Violet read:

"Somebody's been sleeping in my bed and here she is!"

"Who are you?" said the Papa Bear.

"I am Goldilocks," said Goldilocks.

"I'm just right!" interjected Goldi.

Miss Violet smiled right at Goldi.

In first grade, she felt like any other "normal" kid. She could ride her bike without training wheels, hold hands with the toddler in the neighborhood to help them across the street, and tell her brother Henry to make a good choice if he was about to burp at the dinner table.

At seven years old, Goldi still didn't know she was autistic. But the day at recess, when she was chatting with some kids on the monkey bars, and mostly talking about Goldilocks and The Three Bears, something happened:

"Momma Bear made some porridge and it was really too hot!" she exclaimed.

"We know," Max said, "We don't really want to talk about Goldilocks."

"I know it's really the way," Goldi said, "But you can't do it all the time,"

The kids half understood Goldi's response. Max was first to change the subject:

"Why are cornfields the best listeners?" he asked

A riddle made Max feel pretty smart stumping his friends with a mysterious question.

"Well, do you give up?" Max asked looking at their puzzled faces.

All the kids paused.

"We give up," said Bernice.

"Because they're all ears!"

Giggles and laughter followed. Goldi loved the sound and mustered up the biggest belly laugh. More than anything she too wanted to be the one to make them laugh.

"Why did the rooster cross the road?" she asked.

There was no answer.

"He wanted a cheeseburger!" she said giggling.

There were blank stares.

"That doesn't make any sense," Bernice said.

Goldi froze in confusion. She turned away from the kids, chewing on her necklace and flapping. For the first time, she felt a lonely kind of different.

Chapter 3 Papa Bear

Your Father in heaven knows what you need.
Matthew 6:8

Mr. Howard had a good head on his shoulders. He was logical and knew the ins and outs of anything. He had a calm about him even in moments of Goldi's sheer meltdown. Like the time, she was told that her favorite pink baby blanket had to be washed and she would not be able to sleep with it for one night.

"I need it! I need it now!" Goldi screamed. The door slammed and slightly muted the piercing screams. Yet, Mrs. Howard feared a neighbor would call the police for neighborly disturbance. Mr. Howard stood outside her bedroom door.

"Goldi, I'm here," he assured, "I know you are mad. It's going to be okay."

With logic and a calm demeanor, he was able to teach Goldi all the 1, 2, 3's that she needed for unlocking daily mysteries, like zipping her coat, putting a stamp on an envelope, or washing your hands in order to prevent germs. It was to his credit that Goldi was developing a "can do" attitude when she put on all the layers of snow clothes all by herself or was confident of making her own piece of toast.

He knew that raising a daughter like Goldi would indeed be like a walk in the woods. He knew that they would often need to take things one day at a time. He knew the woods would be dark and scary at times. But Goldi had a happy go lucky spirit, and with that the walk in the woods would be a real adventure.

One summer, the family went on a bike excursion on a trail along the river. Goldi rode on a tandem bike with her father. She pedaled at times, then coasted to listen to the gentle water. It was a relaxing ride until suddenly she dragged her feet.

"Goldi, pedal." Mr. Howard told her.

"No! Stop!" she cried.

"We're going further."

"I can't." Goldi insisted.

Mr. Howard looked at his trip meter. It read 5 miles. There was 5 more to go. His natural urge was to take a water break and keep riding.

"Take a drink," he said handing her the water bottle.

Goldi took a small quick sip and handed it right back.

"So lovely here!" Mrs. Howard exclaimed.

"Dad, how fast were we going?" Henry inquired.

"I would say a nice, easy speed. Let's move on." he said pushing his foot on the top pedal.

"No! I'm staying!" Goldi announced swinging her leg off the bike and running towards the river.

"Goldi!" shouted her mother. "Don't go in that river!"

Goldi was too far off. She had stripped off her socks and shoes and left them on the trail. Tip toeing on river rocks, she did not stop until her feet were immersed in the clear water. She found one large sized rock that provided the perfect stage where the river ripples massaged her feet. She raised her arms out feeling the wind hug her. She closed her eyes and breathed a wide smile.

Henry joined Goldi. Mr. and Mrs. Howard sat on a large rock on the river shore.

"The river IS very beautiful," Mr. Howard said looking at Goldi.

"Absolutely breathtaking!" remarked Mrs. Howard.

The family rode 10 more miles that day seeing more tall trees and wild flowers than they could count.

Chapter 4 Momma Bear

As a mother, comforts her child, so I will comfort you. Isaiah 66:13

When Goldi was diagnosed, Mrs. Howard's dreams of sugar and spice and everything nice vanished.

She longed to comb her daughter' beautiful golden hair and dress it up with bows. But after practically wrestling her to the floor to do so, Mrs. Howard gave in to Goldi's wind combed look.

She had tried for something both normal and also nice by setting the dining room table for a tea party. There was lemonade and cookies. All of Goldi's dolls had a place at the table. When Goldi came for tea, she proceeded to take all of her dolls and put them back in their proper place in her room. She took one small sip of lemonade, shoved three cookies in her mouth, and twirled around leaving a scattering of crumbs.

When Goldi went to her first birthday party, Mrs. Howard hoped for a chance at something normal dressed up in fun. But when one balloon accidentally popped, Goldi screamed and insisted on going home immediately. She covered her ears the whole ride home repeating "No Popping! Too loud!"

Every time Mrs. Howard brought Goldi to therapy, she had high hopes. Miss Suzanne had many Firsts and Thens: First you squeeze toothpaste on your toothbrush, then you brush in circles on your teeth. First you sit down, then you eat your lunch. When Miss Suzanne promised a story, Goldi was excited.

But they were not the exciting fairy tales she loved. They were stories called "social stories." They were stories about following the rules at school, or saying hello to a friend, or going to the dentist, and things that didn't start with 'Once upon a time'.

Yet, Goldi followed the rules, she could brush her teeth well and left just as much of a toothpaste glob in the sink as her brother Henry. She sat down at lunch and stayed in her chair. Even though she was scrunched up instead of feet on her floor, this was better than many other kids who jumped around at lunch. She didn't look at people in the eye to say hello but neither did anyone else she noticed. Many people were looking at their smart phones instead of people's faces. Mrs. Howard wore a maybe smile that said, "Maybe things could be close to normal."

Her maybe smile helped to hide worries about the future.

Then one day, after doing many chores, Mrs. Howard took Goldi to the store to buy a new Barbie. Goldi snagged the right one off the shelf as soon as she saw it. Mrs. Howard grabbed some other things and with a heavy load reached the check out. Goldi held her Barbie so tightly, Mrs. Howard had to pry out of her hands to get it scanned by the cashier.

"Your total is 65 dollars even." the cashier said waiting.

As, she searched her purse, Mrs. Howard made an awful discovery.

"I'm sorry, I've left my credit card at home!" she told the cashier.

The cashier agreed to hold her items at the store's front desk until Mrs. Howard returned with the money.

"No!" shrieked Goldi as soon as she realized what was happening.

Determined to avoid a scene, Mrs. Howard quickly grabbed her daughter's hand and walked briskly away.

"We need to get Barbie!" Goldi screamed.

"First, we go home to get the money, then we come back to get Barbie." Mrs. Howard said sounding exactly like Miss Suzanne.

Goldi wasn't going to comply. Over all the beeps, bag rustlings, and even the store announcement for half off Macaroni and Cheese, Goldi's screaming caused shoppers to look with disgust. The door out seemed far away. Mrs. Howard sighed heavy when they reached the car.

"We will be right back! Barbie will be waiting." she said trying to assure Goldi.

"That was MY Barbie!" Goldi shrieked.

There was no reasoning with her nor any peace until they returned, and Goldi held Barbie.

"I sure would like a nice normal day just once!" shared Mrs. Howard to Mr. Howard exhausted from the whole situation.

After the long hard ordeal, Mrs. Howard's maybes were being buried in probably not.

Chapter 5 The Baby Bear

John 13:34 Love one another as I have loved you.

Goldi was Henry's only sibling to bug. Once he jumped on her bed and stole one of her Barbies that lay lined up neatly in a row on her bedroom floor. He kept it hidden in his room and left a note:

"I have your Ballerina Barbie, if you want her back leave 10 pieces of candy at my door."

Goldi knew instantly that she was missing. She tore up her whole room and crumpled up the note.

"She's gone! Where is she?!" she yelled.

Henry felt blamed and shamed for doing something he thought was normal, pesky, little brother stuff. He wished Goldi were like other older siblings, who modelled how to do all the important stuff like ride a bike or lose a tooth. Goldi's firsts had so much quirkiness, he didn't know if he should be excited for them or wish them quickly away.

There were all sorts of feelings that went with having a sister like Goldi. He was frustrated when they got all the way to the circus only to go home because the lions were "too loud" and the elephants were "too stinky". He was mad when Goldi refused to go roller skating because the lights were too bright, and the music was too thundery. He was embarrassed when Goldi talked in circles in front of the neighbor kids about mailboxes and made no sense at all.

Many times, *patience* and *understanding* were the words his parents used. But he didn't know how to be patient when the screaming lasted so long, and they had to miss out on so much fun.

The reason for Goldi being not normal was never explained to him. Henry heard the word *autistic* and thought he was smart enough to figure it out for himself. He knew his brain was normal, and hers was not. Once he offered the perfect solution,

"Just turn that autism part of your brain off. Then, no one will know you have it. " he told Goldi.

"I don't have autism!" Goldi shouted back.

"Do you even know what autism is?" Henry questioned.

"Just stop!" Goldi demanded.

"You are SO annoying!" he said stomping off.

Sometimes, Henry just wanted a break from all the annoyances of autism. But he knew if he did that it meant forgetting he had a sister. When he played football with friends out in the yard, it felt so wonderfully normal. He could throw a long pass, score a touchdown and tackle someone without being distracted from someone screaming on the sidelines.

At night, he often had dreams of catching a bullfrog and showing it to her by holding it right in her face. Her scream was pleasantly defensive instead of horribly devasting. He dreamed that Goldi would actually fight back when he stole her Ballerina

Barbie by beating on his door with a water balloon. Those dreams made him believe that deep down the real Goldi was waiting to come out.

He suspected his parents had some secret that they were keeping until someday. But smart as Henry was, he would have it long figured out before someday came. He had thought that perhaps, he would be the one to one day spill the beans on what was really up with Goldi.

"Goldi has autism. Autism is something that makes you weird and annoying things. But you can't help it because part of your brain isn't working right," he would explain.

Henry had bad dreams too. Dreams of being chased or trying to escape the deep dark woods. When Henry had one, he would walk into Goldi's room, and look at her sleeping. Then, he would lie beside her and each time, Goldi held his cheeks close to hers and pat his head and say, "It's alright Baby Bear." Henry would just close his eyes, nuzzle his nose under Goldi's chin, and say "Ok."

Chapter 6 Just Right Porridge

You shall do what is right and good in the sight of the Lord, that it may be well with you
Deuteronomy 6:8

In the spring of Goldi's first grade year, the Howards were to attend a meeting to discuss their daughter's IEP.

"Why do you have to go to a meeting? What did I do?" Goldi asked with concern.

"You have done a lot of good things!" Mrs. Howard assured.

"No worries, we are going to talk about what is just right for our Goldilocks!" said Mr. Howard with a wink, "Just like that porridge she ate!"

"Of course!" said Goldi.

The Howards sat down at a large rectangular table along with teachers and specialists. They would meet with school staff every year. The table was scattered with pens, paper, notebooks, and stacks of official forms. It seemed that as soon as they hit the chair, a constant clicking of computer keys started to record every word that was said.

"Thank you for coming. School plans for these special needs kids take time. Your ideas are appreciated," said Mrs. Wilson.

"It has been such a delight to have Goldi in our classroom!" Mrs. Crumb, the first-grade teacher said with a wide smile.

"She's our Goldi!" said Mr. Howard.

Both parents had a warm feeling about Mrs. Crumb and the others. They seemed to care less about normal and more about enjoying Marigold for who she was.

"We will begin by telling you all about the wonderful progress Goldi has made this year so far," said Mrs. Wilson.

The mention of Goldi playing with others, being creative, and following the rules so well, caused them both to breathe a sigh of relief.

"Now, we will share some goals with you for Goldi for the coming second grade year." Informed Mrs. Wilson.

As they listened, Mr. Howard took some notes. Mrs. Howard sighed a little bit. Sometimes when it came to setting goals for Goldi, it was a reminder that not only did she have autism, but it always brought up the fact that there are so many things that ▓▓ she **didn't** do yet and needed to do. The Howards agreed to the goals and signed on the dotted line.

Everyone was so hungry when they arrived home. Mrs. Howard began to scurry around the kitchen.

"I'll make porridge!" Goldi said.

Mrs. Howard hesitated a bit. Not wanting more of a mess in her kitchen. Before she could stop Goldi, there was already a big pot on the stove filled with water.

"When is that porridge going to be ready? I'm as hungry as a bear!" said Mr. Howard

"Don't worry dad, it will be ready in no time!" reminded Goldi.

Mrs. Howard turned on the stove on as Goldi stirred the water.

Goldi moved confidently, going straight to the refrigerator for some baby carrots.

"I need to put these in," she said dumping in the whole bag.

After a while the pot was boiling.

"Almost perfect!" Goldi declared.

Mrs. Howard smiled.

"Is there something else you need? The chicken is almost ready." said Mrs. Howard

"Well…. "Goldi thought, "Some salt, pepper, a little bit of chicken broth, garlic, and do we have any corn?"

"Coming right up!" said Mrs. Howard.

Goldi also put in a few potato chips and some crackers.

"Smells delicious!" exclaimed Mr. Howard who had followed the scent into the kitchen, "What do you call it?"

"Just right porridge Dad!" said Goldi.

When they all sat down at the table, Goldi watched as her family took a sip of her creation.

"Well, what do you think?" she asked.

"Tasty!" said Mr. Howard.

"Just right!" said Mrs. Howard. "How did you get the recipe?"

"I guess it doesn't taste so bad, for being a bowl of junk!" said Henry smirking.

I know how to make porridge just right!" exclaimed Goldi, "I really know!"

Chapter 7 Goldi meets Goldilocks.

For in Christ Jesus, you are all sons of God through faith. Galatians 3:26

Soon after the school IEP was signed, sealed, and ready for second grade, Mrs. Howard took Goldi for another evaluation from Dr. Peters. They hadn't seen him since the day of Goldi's diagnosis. Things had certainly changed since then. Goldi was talking up a storm. She was enjoying her teacher at school and all the first-grade activities. Things seemed as close to normal as they could hope for now.

As second grade drew near, they hoped Dr. Peters would remark on how much she had accomplished. Deep down, Mrs. Howard was hopeful that he would say that she had outgrown her autism.

 The waiting room was big, open, bright, and cold. At 8:00 am, there was a bustling of people. Goldi giggled as she and Henry chased each other around the puzzle table. Suddenly, something made them stop in their tracks.

A mother and her daughter had seated themselves close by. The mother held her daughter's hand. Goldi began to stare. The girl was sitting all hunched over in a wheel chair. Goldi could see that not only was her hair golden like hers, but her eyes were blue. But hers had no sparkle. They were open, but they looked so far away. While they waited, her mother held her hand and read a magazine.

The girl in the wheel chair didn't talk or move. She just sat there. As Goldi watched closely, she wondered if the girl was real, for breathing seemed the only thing that made her different than a statue.

"Who is that girl?" Goldi asked.

"Someone." answered her mother, "Someone just right, like you."

Goldi watched some more with fascination. The girl's hair was wind combed just like hers. She wore a pink wrinkly shirt and her socks scrunched up at the bottom just like they did on Goldi's ankles.

"Come on Goldi! Chase me!" cried Henry.

Goldi still didn't move so Henry yanked on her arm.

They continued their chase until they heard a moan.

Goldi stopped chasing Henry and stood frozen. Henry had already found himself a 100-piece puzzle and wasn't paying attention. But to Goldi there was something about this girl that made her wonder.

The girl's moaning grew louder and many people started to look towards the girl in the wheelchair.

Goldi didn't just look. She stared.

"What is she saying?" asked Goldi beginning to be afraid. She had grabbed her mother's arm and held it hard enough she nearly pinched it.

"Goldi, it's okay!" Mrs. Howard said gently prying Goldi's hand off.

"But I am afraid mom!" said Goldi. "She's scary"

The girl moaned again. Her mouth wide open this time. The sound seemed to bounce off the walls.

"Shhh!" the girl's mother said rubbing her daughter's hand.

Mrs. Howard tried to distract Goldi by pointing out the pretty blue fish in the huge aquarium display. But the moaning grew louder and louder.

"Too scary!" Goldi cried "Too loud!"

Mrs. Howard sat Goldi on her lap. She was slightly embarrassed that Goldi didn't understand. This girl had autism too. But she wasn't talking. She wasn't walking. She wasn't able to jump and play. Goldi was more normal than this girl. Goldi knew it and was scared.

"Shh!" she whispered in Goldi's ear. "She can't help it."

The girl moaned again and began to pound a little bit on the arm of her wheelchair. The moaning and pounding grew louder and louder. Everyone in the waiting room did their best to block the sound out.

"Too loud! Too scary!" Goldi repeated "Why does she keep doing that?"

"She is saying something to her mom. Her mother understands." Mrs. Howard trying to assure her.

The moaning kept on for quite some time which made them both wish the wait was over, and their name would be called.

"When will she stop?" asked Goldi putting her hands over her ears.

The answer was unknown, and Mrs. Howard felt so helpless not knowing. Suddenly, the moaning did stop. Goldi and her mother watched as the girl's mother had gently pressed her face against her daughter's. She was kissing her forehead and whispered sweet nothings right into her ear. Suddenly the girl smiled. Her eyes no longer looked far away. Her eyes looked into her mother's eyes and sparkled. She sat taller. She smiled wider and flapped a little.

"Goldi" announced a voice. "Goldi looked up at a woman with a badge."

"Dr. Peters will see you," she said.

Mrs. Howard nudged Goldi off her lap.

"Let's go Goldi," she said grabbing her hand.

The badged woman held one of the double flappy doors open for Mrs. Howard and Goldi.

"Let's go to room 5 here on the left," the woman said pointing.

"Golid!" said another voice.

Goldi stopped walking. *Why was her name being called again?*

"Goldi, we will go to room 6," another badged woman instructed.

Goldi looked. The girl in the wheelchair was being wheeled toward the flapping doors too.

"Goldi?" said Goldi to the girl as she got closer, "You are Goldi too?" she asked.

The mother stopped the wheelchair so that the girl and Goldi were face to face.

The girl wasn't looking right at Goldi. Goldi wasn't looking right at her. But Goldi was flapping and smiling. The girl in the wheelchair making a sound that this time was more like a hum. Her eyes sparkled and she smiled back at Goldi and flapped her hands too.

The two Goldi's walked side by side down the hallway.

"See you later Goldi!" Goldi said waving as she went into room 5.

The girl hummed and smiled as she went into room 6.

Chapter 8 Dreams are wishes your heart makes....

Now faith is the assurance of things hoped for, the conviction of things not seen. Hebrews 11:1

By second grade, leaving the regular classroom for help in the Autistic Room was routine for Goldi. But whenever she left, she felt the weight of stares behind her back. Her classmates knew the first time they met Goldi that she was different. They knew when she walked in line with the class and stepped on the heels of the person in front of her. During math when adding, she just randomly wrote down numbers that looked important. They knew when she would not stop jumping when their teacher, passed out brand new pencils and a box of markers to each student. They knew when Goldi paced after the teacher told them that music class was suddenly cancelled, and they would have to work on their writing journals instead.

The class had heard the word *autistic* when they overheard the Autistic Teacher speaking with their classroom teacher. Autism was an everyday word to Goldi. She knew it to be a part of her world as much as saying "Good Morning." She had heard that word spoken so much that she began to wonder not only what it meant but why her name was always connected to the word. For the time being, it was a mystery to her that left her just wondering.

She kept wondering one night when lying in bed and wasn't able to fall asleep. She wondered why she left her second grade classroom every day at 1 o'clock. She wondered why Miss Suzanne, her therapist, repeated First and Then over and over whenever she had therapy. She wondered why her parents whispered sometimes, looking puzzled, and so serious. She wondered if *autism* meant something amazing or it was something so horrible, one was to keep it secret. Finally, she went to sleep.

Then Goldi was awake. It seemed like she had just fallen asleep. Yet she wasn't the least bit tired. She looked around. Where was she? She wasn't in her bed. She wasn't even in her own house! All her eyes saw was light. Even though she had no idea where she was, she didn't seem to care. The light illuminated a kind of beauty that she had never seen before.

There were flowers all around. The grass below her feet was lush and green. You could see the trees reaching up and burst with deep green leaves and colorful blossoms. The song of the birds whispered in the distance like a lullaby. Goldi hoped the happy melodies would never stop.

Suddenly she saw a deer leap across her path. Though it surprised her, it didn't upset her, it only made her catch her breath and smile. The deer stopped to look at her. Goldi walked a little closer. The deer was still and seemed to smile at her with deep sparkling eyes. Goldi smiled back. She was nearly close enough to touch the tip of its head. As soon as she did, she felt a softness that was indescribable. She had no fear of the deer at all. She had no worries. She neither felt the need to flap or pace. She didn't feel the need to jump with excitement at all the beauty. It was a delightfully different feeling.

Wherever she walked, there was light. It sparkled and glowed and showed off all the beauty around her. Walking further, she saw kids at play. They swung from trees and ran barefoot through the grassy carpet. They were smiling and laughing and singing. As they did, the light that shone, grew more and more brilliant making everything around her, more and more beautiful. The trees continued to bud. The flowers continued to bloom. The sky became bluer with each glance.

Goldi realized something amazing had happened to her. She didn't know what it was. But it was a feeling unlike anything she felt. The light was never too bright. The bird's song wasn't too loud. Though the place was so unfamiliar, it wasn't too scary to be there. Everything was more than just right. It was perfect place. It was a peaceful place.

Then, the light touched her with warmth that gave her a happiness that was nothing like she had ever felt.

"Goldi!" said a deep gentle voice, "Goldi, you are just right! You are perfectl! You are mine!" it said.

Goldi looked up and tried to see a face to match the voice. But all she could see was the beauty that the brilliant light showed her.

"Goldi," whispered a different voice, "Time to wake up."

Though the warm feeling was still with her, she didn't feel the same peace she had felt standing in the light.

"Goldi," said the voice, "Time to get dressed. "

After she wiped the sleep from her eyes, she could see her mother at her bedside. She had left that beautiful place.

"What's going on?" she asked.

"It's Tuesday." Said her mother.

"Oh."

"It's a school day," said her mother.

"I know," said Goldi in a sad sort of tone.

She wished she could climb back in her bed and close her eyes. It was the only way to get back into that wonderful place where she felt so beautiful and peacefully perfect.

In a blink she was in the lunchroom hearing all the conversations about Halloween and the costume parade. It was only a few weeks away.

Soon the whole school would be transformed into a world of mystery. A week before Halloween, Goldi was changing her mind about her costume choice every five minutes. She was thinking not only about her costume but the dream she had the night before. She remained hushed about it. Yet, she didn't want to forget it.

"I still don't know what to be for Halloween!" Goldi said to her mother.

"You can be anything you want to be," said her mother "a fairy, peacock, a ballet dancer, …. maybe you could be Goldilocks!"

"No! I want to be new!" Goldi cried.

"I'm not sure what costumes are still in the stores. The choices might be limited," said her mother.

"Someone new!" Goldi repeated.

Goldi's mother sighed.

"Even dressed in a costume, you'll always be you," she said softly.

"I'm different! I'm not just right! I have to go to that other classroom. I have to work with Miss Suzanne. Why do I have to? I want to be someone new! "Goldi cried.

"Come here," her mother said patting a seat on the sofa.

Goldi willingly sat down.

"You have help so that things are just right for you. You like things just right. Just like Goldilocks! Nothing too cold or hot for her. Nothing too hard or soft. You are our Goldi. YOU are just right. "Mrs. Howard insisted.

"But I really do want to be new!" Goldi cried. She never thought that being just right would also make her feel so different.

"I have a story for you," Mrs. Howard said.

The word 'story' made Goldi eagerly listen.

"Once there was a beautiful girl named Cinderella," her mother began.

"She must be just right!" Goldi determined.

"Everything was not just right, "her mother informed "She was dressed in rags, she had to scrub the floor, wash the windows, dust the shelves, cook the meals, do the laundry, and sleep on the floor by the fire cinders."

Goldi marveled at her mother's story and the parts about the fairy godmother, the ball, and the handsome prince.

"Together Cinderella and her Prince lived Happily ever after!" Mrs. Howard ended.

"Happily, ever after?" Goldi asked.

"Yes. She was dirty and dressed in rags. But then, she became a princess. She became someone new forever after," Her mother said smiling.

Goldi was inspired. If Cinderella could be new as a princess, she could too! At the school parade, in a sparkling blue gown and tiara. Goldi waltzed along. She bumped into Leo the Lion and stepped on Rapunzel's long flowing hair with her clear plastic shoes. But all that mattered was the happily ever after dream stirring up inside of her.

Then after seeing a Disney commercial, Goldi learned that if you wrote to a princess, they would write back. If she were going to be a real princess, this was a way to find out how. Goldi wrote her first letter to Cinderella:

Dear Cinderella,

I have golden hair. I love to swing and walk barefoot. I want to be a Princess.

From,

Goldi

Goldi addressed the letter:

Cinderella

The Castle

Far Away Kingdom

USA

She placed a stamp in the corner and put it in the mailbox with the flag up.

Mrs. Howard found the letter. She knew Goldi's imagination was healthy. She still believed in the

Tooth Fairy, the Easter Bunny, and Santa Claus. Perhaps, she could help her believe in her dream of being a princess. Mrs. Howard wrote back:

Dear Goldi,

I am sure your hair is beautiful. Do you like to wear ribbons, bows, or crowns?

Sincerely,

Cinderella

Mrs. Howard put the letter in an envelope with a shiny gold interior and closed it with a shiny seal.

She addressed it in fancy calligraphy: Miss Marigold Howard, 6607 Creekside Drive. Then she placed a stamp in the corner and mailed it at the post office.

Mrs. Howard enjoyed keeping her secret. The letters were fun to write. She felt she was the perfect person to help nurture this "little princess".

Dear Cinderella,

Bows and crowns are too pinchy. Ribbons can be scratchy. Can I still be a princess?

From,

Goldi

Dear Goldi,

I am sure you have a dress that twirls. Those are the best for dancing.

From,

Cinderella.

Dear Cinderella,

I do like to twirl, but sometimes I trip and fall. Can I still be a princess?

From,

Goldi

"It **is** all pretend," she admitted to Mr. Howard. "Maybe it's going too far. How long until she realizes Cinderella is all pretend? Then how will she keep dreaming?" Mrs. Howard asked her husband.

"The best dreams are the ones that we think are never possible. Some of those dreams really do come true." said Mr. Howard.

Mrs. Howard decided the letter writing had gone on long enough. The next letter she would write would be her last, but it would also be the best one of all. She did some thinking about what she would write while lingering and browsing around a department store. She wasn't looking for anything in particular. There were a lot of interesting new things that caught her eye. But after some time, right before she might have left the store empty handed, she saw something extraordinary in the household item section. It was a most unique clock. Its face was pink with roses. The frame was golden. At the center of the face it said:

It's always time for.... Then circling the face of the clock, in fancy lettering, were the most beautiful words: love, joy, peace, patience, kindness, goodness, faithfulness, gentleness, self-control. At the bottom of the clock it read: These make time precious! Mrs. Howard promptly bought the clock, wrapped it up in pearly white paper and tied it with a silky pink ribbon. The she wrote the longest letter ever.

Goldi found a package sitting on the doorstep with a letter attached.

Mom! "she shouted running into the kitchen. "There's a package AND a letter from Cinderella!

Mrs. Howard smiled at the sound of Goldi's excitement.

"What does the letter say?" raising her eyebrows.

Goldi opened the letter and read:

Dear Goldi,

To be a real princess, you don't need a sparkly dress or the right toes for dancing. You don't need bows in your hair or shiny necklaces. A real princess is someone who helps those in need. That's what love is. She smiles at someone who is sad. She can be counted on to be a friend.

52

That is sharing joy, kindness, and faithfulness. She knows that good things come to those who wait. That's true patience. She does not get angry at others but tries to be a friend first. That is real self- control. She is brave enough to do good in this world because she knows there is not enough good in it. That is real goodness. She shows gentleness to those who are weak. Here is the truth: There is a real King who lives in the most beautiful Kingdom, where princes and princesses live happily forever after! He is the most kind, gentle, loving, patient, faithful, good, and strong King of all. Long ago, He rescued all the princesses and princes in the world because they were far from being good. He rescued them because He loves them so much. When He returned to His kingdom, He left His power with anyone who believed He was the true King. If you believe this to be true, then the King's power is with you and one day you will be a perfect princess in His Kingdom and live happily forever after.

This clock is a gift for you. When I was dancing at the ball with the prince, I wanted time to stop so that I could be a princess forever. When the clock struck twelve, I knew my time as a princess was over. When I married the prince, I became a princess and I did live happily ever after! But I also knew that the King of all Kings, was making me His princess all along, even when I was dressed in rags! All I had to do was to believe it with all of my heart.

Whenever, you look at the clock, think of being a princess. The words on the clock will help you remember how. The King's Spirit, which is His power, will help you. When you feel His power and love in you, that is when you will feel like a princess. And one day, a time will come, when the King will make you a perfect princess that will live happily forever after. But you must believe this with all of your heart.

Sincerely,

Cinderella

"Is this true?" she inquired. "Is there a real king?"

"Yes," answered her mother.

"Where do they live?" Goldi asked.

"Many places all around the world: Sweden, Belgium, Denmark, Spain."

"Which King will make me a real princess?"

"None of those kings will," her mother answered in a serious tone.

"But it says a real KING will make me a princess!" insisted Goldi.

"This king lives in a kingdom that we can't see on the map, but he is still real."

"But.... Cinderella says he came into the world."

"He did a long time ago. Before you and I were even born! Before he went back to His Kingdom, he told everyone he would give them the power to become royal. The King is with them always by this great power and love. If you believe He is the true king. He is with you. He said that one day, anyone who loves Him and believes in Him could be a prince or princess one day and live in His Kingdom forever. His Kingdom is the most beautiful place you could imagine."

Goldi stood listening to her mother and as she spoke her eyes grew big. Her eyebrows jumped up. A beautiful place we cannot even imagine. Just like the dream she had. She hadn't told anyone about it. How did her mother know?

"I know about that place! I do!" Goldi exclaimed.

Goldi's mother came over and rubbed her back. She looked at her with watery eyes. Goldi wondered why she didn't look surprised or why her mother didn't ask her to tell how she knew about such a place. She just smiled and whispered:

 "You can keep dreaming like that and believe that one day being in that beautiful Kingdom with the true King it will not be a dream anymore, it will be true." answered Mrs. Howard.

"I do believe! I promise I believe!" shouted Goldi jumping up and down and twirling.

 She put all of her letters in the music box with the ballerina. Every so often she took out the letters and read them. Each time, her happily ever after dream grew stronger. Goldi put her clock in a place in her bedroom where she could see it as soon as she awoke. Every morning, she looked at the clock and whispered, *"Time to be a princess."*

The night of the Second Grade Christmas Program, snow fell like mad.

"Let's put on the sparkle dress." she suggested "You'll look just like a princess."

"I don't want to!" Goldi yelling and not being princess like at all.

She had no intention of going out on a snowy night just to stand in front of many people looking at her and singing under bright, blinding lights.

"Everyone wants to see you on stage." Mrs. Howard reminded her.

"I DON'T want to go!" Goldi emphasized screaming and stomping her feet.

The car ride was filled with siren blaring NO's. Goldi's face was red with beads of sweat. Her eyes sagged.

"Maybe we should just" turn around and go home," Mrs. Howard said to Mr. Howard. "It's just not worth it. "

"Hey! There's Maggie!" a voice shouted suddenly from the backseat as they pulled into the parking lot. "And James, and Patricia, and Marco! Hey! I'm here!" Goldi called knocking on the car window.

The trauma had vanished like a light turned off. Soon, Goldi stood on stage waving a golden scarf, bouncing with life.

"Joy to the World, the Lord has come! Let earth, receive her King!"

A standing ovation followed. Mr. and Mrs. Howard had tears of joy.

When spring came, the class went to a local farm to go horseback riding. When the horses arrived in the arena with their guides, there was an immediate scramble to be first.

"Take turns!" warned their teacher Mrs. Jenkins.

"Horses are too smelly and big!" Goldi noted backing away.

"We aren't going to just stand here!" said her mother who had volunteered to chaperone, "You're riding a horse!"

"I won't!" shouted Goldi petting her sensory necklace.

Then, tantrum and meltdown collided. Mrs. Howard insisted. Goldi resisted. The noise grew louder. The second graders watched in silence. Even the horses looked as though they were wondering which one would have to carry Goldi kicking and screaming.

"Let's get in line." said Mrs. Howard grabbing Goldi's hand and dragging her to the fence.

"They're such sweet horses," said the leader. "This is Chloe. Say 'hello'".

Goldi became a statue. Mrs. Howard put Goldi's hand on Chloe's mane, then guided it up and down.

"What a nice horse!" she said.

"No!" cried Goldi with tears.

After snickers, pointing, and a few name callings, Mrs. Jenkins called a class huddle.

"Think of how you would feel being told to do something you feared doing, "she said, "We have to cheer for Goldi! "Mrs. Jenkins insisted.

Whether the kids cheered because they were told to, or because they realized how huge it was for Goldi to ride a horse, their courage boost drowned out the screaming as she rode the horse around the entire arena. When she reached the gate, she was all smiles.

"I rode a horse!" she announced climbing off.

Mrs. Howard had tears of joy once again. Her maybes were no longer buried in "probably not" and she could almost see them in her dreams of "why not?"

Chapter 9 Lost in the Woods:

Isaiah 41:10 Fear not, for I am with you, be not dismayed, for I am your God, I will strengthen you, I will help you, I will uphold you with my righteous right hand.

Goldi felt at home in the woods, just like Goldilocks. Sometimes, other girls would come and join her. Goldi assigned them the roles of The Bears while she was always Goldilocks. Then they grew tired of playing the same fairy tale over and over, and soon left her alone to pretend.

Though Goldi was nearing 11 years old, the Howards had shelved the worry of her constant pretending. Fairy tales were as real to her as the nose on her face, and they kept her dreaming of "happily ever after."

Goldi held onto to her childhood by pretending. She pretended before school, after school, and right before dinner. She pretended a lot by talking in different voices to her dolls in her bedroom. They answered back in different voices Goldi gave them.

One evening Mrs. Howard heard only Goldi and wondered why. She walked over to her bedroom door and still heard only Goldi talking in her normal voice. As she leaned her ear to the door, she could hear precisely what Goldi was saying.

"You are very pretty. You look like a princess. I am going to name you Catherine."

Mrs. Howard gently opened the door a crack. Goldi was holding the doll that had been sitting in a rocking chair. The doll Goldi had never seemed to notice. The doll that she hoped Goldi would one day play with just like any other 'normal' girl.

"You are my friend!" Goldi said kissing her doll Catherine's cheek.

The Catherine doll didn't say anything. Goldi just kept on talking and the doll just kept on listening.

"You will be a nice friend!" Goldi said sitting her doll on her lap.

Mrs. Howard watched and smiled with tears streaming down her face.

Goldi watched kids at recess that might be her real friends. She would jump with excitement when they played soccer ball. But she never joined in the game.

One day, someone invited her:

"Kick the ball away from the other team and try to get it in the net," a boy instructed.

Goldi grabbed the ball and threw it across the field towards the net.

"That's against the rules. You have to KICK the ball!" the boy shouted.

Goldi looked down and walked away. The kids shrugged their shoulders and continued to play. She watched how successful they were without her but wished for a second chance.

One night before sleeping, Goldi showed her fourth-grade class picture to Catherine and introduced each classmate.

"Sam likes dogs. Mary Ellen has gymnastics every Thursday. Josh can shoot three baskets in a row. Ben plays the piano. Anna is a good artist. Here I am. But... I am not sure if they know something about me," she said softly.

During lunch period, there was a sea of loud echoes that froze Goldi. The odor was a smear of everyone's lunch. Goldi plugged her nose as she looked around hoping to find another pair of eyes that met hers. She sat down in one empty chair at a table of girls talking about nail polish. No one really acknowledged her except with a look questioning her presence. In the noise and obnoxious smell, she tried hard to turn off the world as she ate, imagining she was in her bedroom, talking to her doll Catherine. The first thing she would tell her was that no one talked to her.

Chapter 10 Goldiella

You shall be a crown of beauty in the hand of the Lord, and a royal diadem in the hand of your God. Isaiah 62:3

On the first day of fifth grade, Goldi walked into room 5-B and sat down next to a girl wearing a T-shirt with the printed words: *I used to be a mermaid* on the front.

"I know a mermaid!" said Goldi to her seatmate.

The girl looked at Goldi with her eyebrows raised.

"You know, a mermaid?" she asked.

"Well, yes, the one that wanted to be human. "Goldi explained.

The girl looked at Goldi in disbelief.

"What?" she said.

"You know, Ariel. The one that wanted to be human so she could meet the prince. Just like Cinderella met the prince at the ball. "Goldi continued.

"What are you talking about?" the girl said shockingly. "Those are both STORIES! Get it?" she snapped.

"Well of course I got it!" Goldi said giggling.

"Ariel Henderson?" Mrs. Babcock, their 5th grade teacher, called out.

Mermaid shirt girl raised her hand.

"You're Ariel?" Goldi shouted. "Wow! …. I can't believe…"

Her excitement bounced her off the chair and jumped repeatedly.

"Easy! Goldi, isn't that your name? asked the teacher.

"Of course, and that's Ariel! She used to be a mermaid!" she answered excitedly.

Laughter burst across the room like a wave. Ariel was pleased to receive attention. Goldi was thrilled to meet Ariel, *who used to be a mermaid*.

"Welcome to 5th grade everyone!" greeted Mrs. Babcock with a smile, "It's going to be a great year. I hope you're all ready to work hard and have fun too. Just think, this is your last year in elementary school, next year you will be in junior high."

The class was silent. They weren't sure how Mrs. Babcock could make thing fun if they had to work hard. But soon, the kids found her to be nice. She winked at Goldi often. She read long stories but did the character voices well which held the kids' attention. She praised the kids often with high fives or knuckles. Mrs. Babcock wore a dress every day. But on her feet, she always wore bright white tennis shoes.

In 5th grade there were reports, reading assignments, writing paragraphs, tests, worksheets, and other things that made Goldi's mind tired and her hand hurt. Learning in Fifth Grade to Goldi meant finding out everything and anything there was to know in the world. So, she really was having fun just as Mrs. Babcock promised.

When they began a unit on the Pilgrims and Indians, Goldi was bright eyed. Mrs. Babcock introduced the unit, "We've been talking about the Pilgrims coming to the New World. When they came, they met some people that were already here, the Native Americans. The Pilgrims and Native Americans were very different from each other. Before we talk about how the two were different, can anyone tell me what the word 'different' means?"

There was silence in the classroom first. Then a boy named Simon raised his hand," It means you are not like anyone else."

"That is true. "replied Mrs. Babcock, "Does anyone else have an idea?"

There was silence again. Goldi was getting impatient and began to flap. She should be the one to say something! Forgetting to raise her hand, she jumped up exclaimed:

"It means that you can be any kind of all the different princesses that you want to be like Cinderella, or Ariel, or any princess you want!"

Goldi jumped up and down many times. She was so thrilled with her answer. Then she noticed the stares around her, she sat down immediately.

The whole class began to snicker. Mrs. Babcock told the class to quiet down and whispers of "Seriously?" followed. Goldi felt her sensory necklace feeling embarrassed. Mrs. Babcock didn't laugh. She didn't frown at Goldi. She just smiled and said

"Good try Goldi."

Soon, *weird* was the word any fifth grader would use to describe Goldi. They could handle walking outside in the snow without their coats on for a fire drill. Goldi insisted on wearing one. They liked all the noise and energy at the school Pep assembly. They all raised their hand to come up to the front to dance with the school mascot. Goldi wore headphones and sat near the doorway to the gym for a quick escape. They thought it extremely annoying that she talked about fairy tales and princesses constantly.

Once when she was working in the Autistic Room, Mrs. Babcock took the opportunity to talk with the class about Goldi.

"Goldi is autistic," Mrs. Babcock explained.

"She does think and act differently than the rest of us. But she is a kid just like you and deserves your kindness. Treat her like you would like to be treated as the saying goes." Mrs. Babcock said looking into all of their eyes. "Any questions?"

All the students felt as though they had heard this speech before. *Be nice to everyone. Everyone is different in their own way. Blah Blah Blah.*

Mrs. Babcock assigned students to sit with Goldi at lunch. When it was Ariel Anderson's turn, she was a bit nervous. She had no desire to be Goldi's friend.

Goldi smiled and sat scrunched up in her chair at the table.

Ariel wondered how Goldi could eat that way.

"What's for lunch?" she asked putting down her lunch tray.

"Well, a soft pretzel, chicken nuggets, chips, and applesauce," said Goldi holding up each food item.

Ariel couldn't think of any other topic of conversation. Goldi just kept on eating and looking around.

"Sorry, you are not a mermaid," said Goldi all of the sudden.

"I told you, they exist only in stories. My full name is Ariel Lucille Anderson. Did you ever hear a mermaid named that? "she asked with raised eyebrows.

"You're lucky your name is Ariel, the name of a mermaid." Goldi replied.

"Why do you talk about fairy tales all the time?" Ariel asked.

"I like fairy tales. There's Goldilocks, Cinderella, and-"

"I get it!" Ariel interrupted, "You are even named after a fairy tale!"

"My name is Marigold Ellanora Howard." Goldi replied confidently, "My mom and dad named me just right!" exclaimed Goldi.

"Exactly! You are Goldi because you have to have everything just right just like Goldilocks. You are Cinderella because you think you are going to turn into some princess and live happily ever after. Your name should be …. Goldiella!"

"Ariel, I told you my name is Goldi! You already know that!" replied Goldi.

"You think everything is a fairy tale. Except this is the real world." Ariel said.

Goldi held Catherine after school and told her what Ariel had said.

"I don't think Ariel likes fairy tales! I wonder why? They all end 'happily ever after'. I sure like that! Maybe Ariel misses being a mermaid?"

Goldi thought about what she could do to help Ariel. She didn't seem happy. In the meantime, she made many other acquaintances in faith grade. Occasionally at recess and lunch, she interacted with them and felt a small sense of belonging.

Those peers thought that if they had sat with Goldi at lunch or played with her at recess, then they had done their good deed for the day. But Gold knew that friendship was more than short bits of time with someone. She knew loneliness more than anyone. More than anyone she wanted a real friend and she knew that the best thing she could do was to follow Princess Cinderella's advice.

"Time to be a princess", she still said every morning. She memorized all the words on the clock that Cinderella had given her.   Each day at school she put them into practice. She a brand-new pencil to her seatmate who only had a stub during journal writing. She purposely went to the back of the line even though she was really thirsty after the mile run in gym class. Maria received a compliment note from Goldi for getting a 100% on her spelling test. She bravely spelled *chrysanthemum* in front of the whole class. She read a poem out loud over the school intercom. The bravest thing she did was to approach a girl standing by herself outside at recess and say

"Hello, would you like to swing with me?"

The girl refused. So bravely, Goldi accepted her refusal, sighed, and walked away to swing on her own.

"The King is making me a real princess!" she whispered, "I have the Spirit of the King."

Each time her toes seemed to touch the sky, she said those words, hoping more and more to really believe them.

Chapter 11 Mean and Ugly Stepsister

Ephesians 4:32 Be kind to one another, tenderhearted, forgiving one another just as God in Christ forgave you.

Ariel Anderson couldn't figure Goldi out. She was annoyed with Goldi's fascination with fairy tales and was grossed out by the way she ate her lunch. To Ariel, autism was something that made Ariel superior to Goldi.

But Goldi wanted to be her friend. She showed more kindness by inviting her to play on the monkey bars at recess when Ariel walked outside alone.

"We could pretend we were real monkeys! "Goldi asked her.

But Ariel didn't answer. She just looked at Goldi coldly. Then she practically had her nose in the air. Goldi shriveled up a little. She didn't know why Ariel wouldn't smile and say something. But she shrugged her shoulders and went out alone allowing the spring breeze to make her happy again.

As she was swinging, Ariel approached her with a few others. Goldi wondered if Ariel had changed her mind about playing with her and dragged her feet to slow down.

"Hey Goldiella!" she said resolving that this was her true name, "You know back when I was a mermaid, I swam with the dolphins!"

Even though there were snickers around her, Goldi was amazed.

"Really? Did you talk with them? What did they say? "she asked with intense interest.

"You know, eeek eeek, squeak squeak, something like that." Ariel replied.

Everyone laughed including Goldi. Ariel and the others walked away realizing how easily you could fool Goldi.

"You sure are lucky Ariel!" Goldi shouted out.

That afternoon, when she was home in her room, Goldi saw the sea shell she had found on the family trip to the ocean. She picked it up and held it to her ears. Goldi always loved the sound she heard. Maybe Ariel really did miss being a mermaid. Maybe giving her the shell would make her happy. Maybe this is what it would take to make Ariel a friend.

The next day, Goldi put the shell on Ariel's desk. Goldi had written a note and laid it beside the shell:

This is for you because it may help you remember when you were a mermaid. From, Goldi

"What's this for?" Ariel asked when she saw it sitting there.

"For you!" declared Goldi. "Tada!"

Ariel just shrugged her shoulders and stuffed the shell in her pocket.

Later, Goldi found it on the floor in the hallway near the lockers.

"Goldi picked it up. Ariel had already packed up her backpack and was walking out the door for the bus.

"Ariel, you dropped your shell!" she yelled running towards her.

Ariel stopped and looked at Goldi.

"Grow up Goldiella! I can't hear anything in that shell!" she said sternly.

Goldi froze holding the shell in her hand.

"Ok Ariel! Thanks for telling me! I'm sorry. I promise I won't ask you more about being a mermaid Ariel!" she shouted.

"Good!" Ariel said walking away.

She brought the shell home and brought it to her ear. She could hear the ocean waves so very clearly.

"Too bad, she doesn't hear it," she told her doll Catherine, "Being a mermaid must have been so amazing!"

Chapter 12 Invitation

Revelation 19:9 Blessed are those who are invited to the marriage supper of the Lamb.

Catherine Danielson sat across the room, in the front row of desks. She had blond hair like Goldi's but it was perfectly combed and styled each day. She was never seen wearing anything twice. It seemed Catherine was like the Teacher's Pet. She was always on time with her homework. She followed all the rules. Mrs. Babcock gave her 100% on many papers. The fifth graders were especially "Wowed" with Catherine because there was a rumor that she was really the great granddaughter of the King and Queen of Thailand. When Goldi heard this, she couldn't wait to tell her doll and became wowed herself that a real princess was right in their classroom.

Catherine was never short of friends. At lunch one afternoon, when Goldi was sitting alone, she overheard her talking to a whole table of friends about a trip to the ocean.

"Last summer, we went to Cumberland Island off the coast of Georgia," Catherine shared, "We actually saw wild horses running along the ocean shore. It was so amazing!"

"I thought wild horses were only out west," said Ariel. "I can't believe you saw horses in the wild on the beach!"

"It's true!" said Catherine in a dreamy voice. "My dad says next time we go back; he'll see if I can actually pet one. Not sure how tame they are. I really want a horse of my own. I've wanted one forever."

Goldi listened and wondered about what she would say, if she were sitting right there with the girls. Catherine had never been assigned to sit with her at lunch. She had never had the courage to approach Catherine even to say "hello". Now, Goldi sat alone, listening to Catherine a *real* princess.

Catherine looked over and made eye contact with Goldi. She noticed the way Goldi scrunched her knees up against the table. She noticed her milk mustache and her wind combed hair. She noticed how her clothes were slightly mismatched. Even though Goldi was in her class, she pretty much ignored her. Goldi blushed, feeling embarrassed that a real princess noticed her. Catherine noticed for a moment, then continued talking to the girls at the table. Goldi looked down and finished her lunch.

Before the weekend, all the 5th grade girls received an invitation to Catherine's Birthday Party. School Policy said "all should be invited" Catherine, the rule follower, included all the girls in the fifth grade including Goldi.

"It's next Saturday at 1 o'clock," Goldi informed her mom.

"It says, the girls are being served lunch at the Flowers Hotel. That's a fancy place." said her mom.

"Like a castle?" Goldi asked.

"I'd say so. Guests are served meals on china plates, and drinks in crystal glasses. There are chandeliers hanging from the ceiling."

"May I go? "asked Goldi.

"Do you want to go??" her mother asked with raised eyebrows.

"Yes!" Goldi said jumping.

"She's going to a party?" Henry asked.

"Yes. "Mrs. Howard said,

"Are they going to play laser tag, or ride go- carts? "he asked.

"They are eating lunch in the ballroom at the Flowers Hotel. "Mrs. Howard informed.

"Well, she'd better not leave crumbs, sit up straight in her chair, and comb her hair, and- "

"Thank you Prince Polite," Mrs. Howard interrupted.

Henry stopped and muttered "Have a good time."

Goldi marked the date on her wall calendar.

At school, every girl in class was talking about the party. Ariel and another girl Maria talked with Goldi at recess.

"Goldiella, are you going to Catherine's party?" asked Ariel.

"Yes! This coming Saturday at 1 o'clock!" she answered.

"Exactly Goldiella! You know you have to dress up? Ariel asked with a smirk.

"Of course!" Goldi told her.

"Don't look all wrinkly Goldi and try to actually comb your hair. Otherwise they may not let you in the hotel, "Maria informed.

"Yeah, there is a dress code, that means... no bunched- up socks and tennis shoes." Ariel said.

 "Whatever." Goldi said. This was the word she had heard many fifth graders say. She had learned when to say it and to say it confidently. It was the word of all words that let others know, that they were not at all bothered by someone's intention to make them doubt, fear, or worry.

Chapter 13 The Fairy Godmother

Look, and see, wonder, and be astounded. For I am doing a work in your days that you would not believe if told. Habakkuk 1:5

On a Wednesday after school, Goldi met with Miss Suzanne for therapy. With Catherine's birthday party coming up in a few days, she was especially eager.

"There's a birthday party on Saturday," Mrs. Howard informed.

"How exciting!" Miss Suzanne said.

"It's at the Flowers Hotel!" Goldi said jumping and flapping.

"Calm hands and feet," said Miss Suzanne gently putting down Goldi's arms. "Tell me about it."

Miss Suzanne put her hands over Goldi's. Goldi wanted to break free, but she knew it was habit that should stop. She couldn't express her excitement without hand flaps and jumps. But she needed to talk like a "normal" person.

"It's going to be very fancy," said Goldi, "So I need to be just like Cinderella."

Miss Suzanne released Goldi's hands and gently nudged her face to meet hers.

"Well, let's see if we can make a princess!" she whispered.

Like always, Miss Suzanne used a lot of firsts and thens:

"First you must walk in the ballroom with a step, step, and stop. Step, step, and stop. Then, you look at someone to see the color of their eyes and say "Hello".

Goldi stepped then hopped a little. Her hello was sweet, but her eye contact was far away.

"Now when you eat, first you take a tiny bite, and then, you chew with your mouth closed."

Goldi bit off half of the practice cookie, and crumbs spilled out.

They practiced these firsts and thens for some time. Goldi could *almost* do it all right.

Then Miss Suzanne told a social story called "*I can have fun at the party.*" Goldi already knew there would be cake and ice cream, and birthday presents, and the Flowers Hotel was much too fancy for balloons popping. There wasn't really anything in the story that Goldi didn't know but she listened as best she could. After working for two hours, Miss Suzanne consulted with Mrs. Howard. Goldi sat in the waiting room staring at a closed door, listening to their voice tones go up and down as they talked.

"She can really do a lot if she puts her mind to it" Miss Suzanne reported.

"Yes, we've noticed some wonderful changes." Mrs. Howard said.

"I know this party is a big deal. Goldi seems very excited."

"She certainly is. I do hope it is a good experience for her," Mrs. Howard said in a concerned tone, "I am trying to believe that the sky is the limit for Goldi. But I am afraid something like this makes the sky seem too far out of her reach."

"I bet Goldi will at least stand on her tiptoes," Miss Suzanne replied.

"Thank you for helping her come this far." Mrs. Howard said.

Miss Suzanne opened the door and looked right at Goldi.

"I hope you have a grand time at the party Goldi!" Miss Suzanne said, "Just remember your manners, and be yourself." she advised.

"Of course, I'm going to be myself!" she exclaimed.

Miss Suzanne waved and watched Goldi twirl all the way to the car.

"Maybe the magic will work for at least one night," Miss Suzanne thought.

Mrs. Howard took Goldi to find a gift for Catherine. Finding something who already had everything seemed impossible. Goldi wasn't thinking of being practical or proper. She passed by the stores at the mall that sold purses, earrings, and makeup, and insisted on the Toy Store. After looking at dolls,

Barbies, and tea party sets. Then something caught Goldi's eye:

"This!" she said pointing.

Mrs. Howard picked up a shiny brown china horse. Its mane looked to made of real horse hair and it had a real leather saddle mounted on the top.

"It's beautiful Goldi, but maybe we should choose something else," her mother pleaded.

"No mom! I heard Catherine say she wanted a horse!" Goldi insisted.

"I am not sure this is the horse she had in mind."

"Mom! I need to give this to Catherine!"

Mrs. Howard complied with hesitation and paid for the horse. At home, Goldi immediately took the horse to her room, sat it on her dresser with the many other figurines. Then she stood back to admire it.

"You're going to be a birthday gift to someone who really wants a horse of her own. Her name is Catherine. She will really like you. You are just right!" she said.

One hour before the party, Goldi wore a pink sequined dress that she had never worn before. Even though the tags were cut off, Goldi still felt the fabric was too scratchy, but being the fanciest thing in her closet, she wore it willingly. Her hair was curled in long slender locks that bounced gently. When Mrs. Howard used hairspray, Goldi squinted and nearly fell over dizzy. Goldi had blotches of pearly pink nail polish all over her fingers that her mother quickly touched up. Finally, Mr. and Mrs. Howard smiled at their young beauty. Her dress was long and flowing. Her shiny white open toe shoes had tiny rose petal bows at the toes. There was a subtle blush to her cheeks and lips, thanks to Mrs. Howard's delicate touch.

"Is it a costume party?" Henry asked.

"Very funny," said Mrs. Howard.

"Here," Henry said holding out a tiny package. "Cinderella should wear this."

Goldi took the package from his hand.

"When Grandma Marigold wore this to fancy concerts and parties, she felt like a real princess." Mrs. Howard explained.

Goldi carefully lifted the lid and dangled a gold necklace in front of her eyes. In the middle of the chain, there was a heart with pink stones that sparkled.

Goldi caressed the worn beads of her sensory necklace.

"Shall we put it on?" Mr. Howard asked.

"Okay," Goldi said "It **is** prettier than this one."

As soon as Mr. Howard took her necklace and set it aside, Goldi felt strange.

"Look at yourself," said Mr. Howard handing her a mirror.

Though the face in the mirror didn't look familiar, the sparkle in her Grandmother's necklace, gave her confidence.

"Just right" she said.

Chapter 14 The Ballroom Party

But let your adorning be the hidden person of the heart with imperishable beauty of a gentle and quiet spirit, which in God's sight is very precious. 1 Peter 3:4

The Flowers Hotel was set in a grassy hill off the main highway. The parking lot was a half a mile away from the Hotel but could be seen visibly in the distance. Guests parked their cars and then took a carriage ride up a brick road through the hotel gardens to the steps of the front entrance. Flowers bloomed all around in the spring and summer making the Hotel a popular place for weddings, parties, and concerts.

Mr. Howard drove into the lot and stopped at the carriage gate.

"Shall I ride with you up to the Hotel?" he asked.

"I'm fine." Goldi told him.

"I'll pick you up at 6 o'clock." he said.

Goldi lifted her dress and stepped out of the car. An empty carriage waited. A suited man with a top hat, took her hand and helped her into the carriage. Goldi sat down on the plush velvet seat and waved at her dad through the window. Mr. Howard waved, and drove away.

The sight of the Flowers Hotel would make anyone believe that fairy tales were real. Goldi never saw so many roses, tall feathery grasses, and fountains. Maple trees and graceful weeping willows were scattered around. The rich green grass carpeted the hilltop where the Hotel stood. When the carriage reached the front steps, she hesitated. The doors had gold panels with coat of arms carvings. The marble steps had a runner of red carpet. Through the glass windows she could see the sparkles of chandeliers. The footmen offered his hand to Goldi and she slowly stepped out, lifted her dress, and walked up the marble stairs. There was a sign with calligraphic writing that read: *Catherine Danielson's Birthday Celebration.* The soft music guided Goldi's steps toward the ballroom where the tables were dressed up with orchids, lilies, and roses. There was a string quartet playing softly on a stage with a sheer, purple curtain backdrop.

Many girls were seated and chatting. When Goldi walked into the room, many stared in her direction. Whispers followed. No one recognized her.

"May I have your name please?" said another suited man.

"Marigold Ellanora Howard," Goldi said slowly.

He offered his arm to her. Goldi wrapped her arm around his and she was escorted to table 6. A chair was slid out for her and a fine white linen napkin was spread on her lap. The gentlemen bowed before leaving.

Goldi could recognize most of the fifth-grade girls at her table. Ariel, Maria, then Patricia, and Mary Anne all had tea cups half full and a fancy china plate of food that looked very much like a work of art.

"Hello," greeted Ariel, "I'm Ariel, are you a friend of Catherine's?"

"Hello, "said Goldi.

"I'm Maria", "Do you know Catherine from school?"

"Yes," said Goldi.

The girls at the table stared at her nearly mesmerized with curiosity. Goldi looked so familiar to them, and yet also so unfamiliar.

"The tea smells delicious," Goldi said.

Slowly she lifted the teacup to her lips.

"Delightful," she said smiling.

"I've never tasted tea like this before," said Patricia.

Mary Anne turned to Goldi.

"Have you ever been to the Flowers Hotel?" she asked.

Goldi gently laid her tea cup down on the saucer and dabbed the corners of her mouth with her napkin.

"I've been here in my dreams." Goldi said in an airy like voice.

The girls nodded and smiled. Goldi beamed.

As they enjoyed a delicious lunch of toasted cheese sandwiches, crisp chips, chocolate covered strawberries, and cinnamon tea, Goldi moved with poise and grace. She took small sips of her tea and tiny bites of her food. She wiped the corners of her mouth frequently sitting straight in her chair with her feet flat and still on the floor. All the while, the girls whispered to each other.

"She won't tell us her name." said Maria

"I don't think I've ever seen her in fifth grade," said Patricia

"She looks just like Goldiella!" said Ariel.

"It couldn't be her. Goldi is way too clumsy and never combs her hair! Besides, her name isn't Goldiella! It's Goldi!" Mary Anne declared.

Goldi overhead all the whispers but said nothing. The girls looked at her with curiosity and she simply smiled.

Catherine had been moving around the room greeting her guest. Her hair was done up with rose tiara that had diamonds. Her sky-blue crystalline dress shimmered.

When she came to the table, she smiled pleasantly at everyone seated.

"Hello everyone," she said.

"Catherine! This sure is elegant!" Maria exclaimed first.

"For sure. This is really being royal." said Ariel

"Wait to you see what's for dessert," Catherine said excitedly. "My mother had the chef make a three-tiered birthday cake!"

Goldi nodded and smiled at Catherine.

"Hello!" said Catherine, politely, not recognizing her either. "I'm glad you came!"

"Thank you," said Goldi softly.

Chapter 15 The Clock Strikes 12

He has made everything beautiful in its time. He has put eternity into man's heart, yet so that he cannot find out what God has done from the beginning to the end. Ecclesiastes 3:11

The curtain on stage opened and a trumpet sounded. Two men in tuxedos pushed the giant three- tiered cake out from the kitchen on a table with wheels.

Catherine's father and mother came out on stage. Mr. Danielson was suited in a white collared shirt, a bow tie, and a black suit coat. Mrs. Danielson looked like a fairy queen draped in gold.

"Let's all sing to our Birthday girl!" said Mr. Danielson.

The string quartet played an introduction. Mr. Danielson gestured to the girls.

As they all sang, the cake was wheeled around for all to see. It was the most beautiful cake the girls had ever seen. White pink roses laced the sides and top. Real ones circled the base with gold jewels.

During the applause, Catherine closed her eyes. For a few silent moments everyone wondered about her secret wish before blowing out the candles. After the remnants of the candle flames floated above, Mr. Danielson said:

"Enjoy the cake!"

The girls at table six all looked down at their piece of cake on a glass plate with a tiny silver fork. One taste set their tongue dancing.

"This is probably is the same cake served at Cinderella's wedding!" she exclaimed Goldi

"You don't say?" said Ariel, "You must really know many fairy tales then," she said winking at Goldi. Just the mention of Cinderella made her certain that Goldi really **was** sitting right there with them.

There was a large gift table near the stage covered with various sized gifts. With her mother's help, Goldi had wrapped Catherine's present in gold paper and tied it with a white silk bow. Catherine sat down in what looked like a throne. All the girls sat waiting for her to open the gift they had given. Ariel had given her a set of nail polishes, lipsticks, and face powders. Maria gave a charm bracelet with rhinestones. Catherine smiled and blew kisses to each gift giver to say, 'thank you'. As the gift table grew bare, it looked as though Goldi's present would be opened last. The long wait made her heart knock wildly against her chest. As soon as Catherine picked up her gift, Goldi wanted to flap her hands she was so excited. But instead, she reached up and gently caressed her grandmother's necklace, when Catherine held Goldi's present and read the card:

"This is something you've always wanted"

Goldi.

Catherine looked closely at the china horse. She looked as though in a shock. She looked around the ballroom for the gift giver but could not identify Goldi in the crowd.

"Ladies!" announced Mr. Danielson, "Please join us outside on the terrace for the presentation our gift to Catherine."

"A toy horses. Really?" Ariel said. "Who gave her that?"

"How embarrassing! Maybe that's what she wanted when she was 5 years old!" snickered Maria.

Goldi's heart sank. Catherine didn't even smile. She just put her horse aside in crumpled up tissue paper. Goldi allowed herself to flap more under the table.

Everyone walked out to the back terrace. It was a large area with a fountain in the middle. Steps lead down to the main grounds full of flower gardens. Goldi lagged behind. She continued caressing her necklace and flapping. But she was a princess, and princesses are to be calm. So, she took a deep breath, and slowly followed the rest outside.

Catherine was instructed to sit down by the fountains with her eyes closed. Her father appeared holding the reins of a chestnut brown horse with a brilliant black mane.

As the clip clop of horse hooves grew closer, Catherine opened her eyes.

"Happy Birthday!" Mr. Danielson said kissing his daughter on the cheek.

Catherine nuzzled against the horse.

"Looks like THAT'S what she really wanted," said Ariel looking at Goldi.

"Let's go pet him," Maria said.

Goldi took backward steps and flapped more, tripping over her long dress and tearing it at the hem.

"Oh, dear," she said softly.

Ariel was so tempted to give away Goldi's secret. But she decided it was not very princess like. She just looked at Goldi with a face that said, *"Get it together."*

While many waited to meet Catherine's horse, a photographer took pictures of guests. Suddenly a suited man appeared playing an accordion with a small monkey on his shoulder. He carried a basket with several long- stemmed roses and small ribbon tied packages.

"Gifts for our guests!" announced Catherine's father.

As the suited man played music on his accordion, the monkey picked up one long stemmed rose from the basket along with a small box. He danced his way over to Ariel and handed it to her.

"That is cutest thing!" she said holding her gifts close.

 Goldi glued her eyes on the monkey as he danced his way around to all the other guests. As he drew closer to her, she began to flap her hands more rapidly as she took more steps backwards. She lost her balance, tripped, and fell near the stairs leading down to the gardens.

"I have to go!" she cried picking herself up quickly.

"Um! Goldiella, the party isn't over yet!" Ariel shouted.

"I'm going!" Goldi shouted, running down the steps tugging at her necklace so forcefully, it fell to ground before she reached the bottom.

Goldi's rapid movement caused the monkey to chase after her.

"Sammy! You come here!" yelled his owner. His accordion squeaked jumbled notes as it fell to the floor.

"Too crazy! Too much!" Goldi cried as she hurried faster away.

Everyone including Catherine watched all the ruckus and saw Goldi rush away.

"Who is that leaving?" she asked her dad.

Her father phoned the footman at the carriage gate.

"One of our guests may need assistance," he informed.

Goldi was soon far away from the party. Nothing would turn her back. When she reached the gate, her necklace was lost, her dress was torn and smudged, and she had tears in her eyes.

"Leaving already?" the footman asked.

"Yes!" Goldi cried.

He offered her some water, and a hand. Goldi climbed eagerly into the carriage, not bothering to be graceful.

"Is someone waiting to take you home?" he asked.

"I need to call my dad," Goldi said in tears.

The footman offered Goldi his phone.

"Dad, please come!" she cried.

When the carriage reached the parking lot, Goldi saw father's car approaching. The ride was quiet. The only noise was the hum of the engine. Within two steps of inside her house, she tore off anything princess, and closed up the world, snug inside her bed.

Chapter 16 Happily Ever After

Outdo one another in showing honor. Romans 12:10

Let each of you look not only to his own interests, but also to the interests of others. Philippians 2:4

Two good nights of sleep before returning to school helped calm her emotions. She dressed on Monday in the first thing she pulled out of her draw; a pair of polka dot pants, and a blue striped t-shirt. She gave her hair a few strokes with a brush and put on her dependable sensory necklace. She had to somehow tell her parents she had lost the necklace. But she didn't know how to tell them anything about the party.

Before breakfast, she took out the letters from "Princess Cinderella," and spread them out on her bed, then picked up each one and read it. She had read them so many times and felt so strongly that dreams could really come true. Now, she felt hopelessness. There was no use in dreaming, so she began to tear each letter up one by one, making a big sprinkle of confetti on the floor.

"Are you ready for school?" asked her mother peering into her room.

"Mom," she said softly, "I have to tell you something."

"What do you want to tell me?"

"It just doesn't work. I can't be a real princess. Being a princess is way too hard!"

Mrs. Howard walked into the room, and immediately saw the mess on the floor.

"What do you mean?" she asked.

"I am a failure. I have heard you say *autism* many times. I know mom. I know I have autism!" Goldi cried.

Mrs. Howard sat down beside her.

"I'm sorry we never talked about it with you. I guess we were waiting until you were older so that maybe you could understand it all better. No matter what though, you are just right! "

"No! I am not! I am different!" Goldi cried.

"Every person is, and all of us have something not right about us."

"I can't have autism and be just right! I've been wishing that one day I would be a real princess. That's just a fairy tale. Fairy tales aren't real!" Goldi shouted with tears.

Mrs. Howard didn't know what to say to make the tears stop. The only thing **to** say was the truth.

"Goldi, you born with autism. But to us, you **were** just right. You loved fairy tales. They helped give you an amazing imagination. And an imagination like that helps you believe in something impossible. Goldi, Cinderella is me. I was the one who wrote the letters."

"What? Mom, why did you do that?" Goldi shouted.

"Because I wanted to keep you wishing and dreaming."

"Well, mom! Let me tell you something. Dreams don't work. They don't come true!"

"Some dreams don't. But this dream will if you believe. The dream I wrote about in the last letter will come true because it's all true!!" Mrs. Howard declared.

"So what you are telling me is that there really is a king who is making me a princess?" Goldi asked with strong suspicion in her voice.

"When you believe He is really the true King, then you have His power."

"Well, I don't have power. I have autism."

"But you have His power, Goldi. Ever since, you were born, I've seen His power in you."

"That doesn't make any sense!"

"So many things that I never thought would happen, DID happen! And it's because of His power in you."

"Whatever!" Goldi said sternly back.

"No Goldi!" insisted her mom "What if?"

"I'm saying Whatever!" argued Goldi with her face red from crying.

"I say, **what if** you never really talked? **What if** you never rode that horse? **What if** you never sang at the Christmas concert? **What if** you never got to 5th grade? **What if** you never went to the Flowers Hotel for a birthday party? What if you never played with your doll or anything or anyone? What if you never made one friend at school? **What if** you **are** going to be more than just right? **What if** someday, you will be a perfect princess? Dr. Peters told us the sky would be the limit. He was only half right. There are **no** limits to what you can do with the King's power in you, Goldi. The King's power IS in you. All your believing in Him showed His power was really in you. He loves you. He is making you a real princess!"

"Stop talking about it!" Goldi shouted. "I don't want to talk about it anymore! I am a failure!"

Mrs. Howard sighed and looked down at the confetti mess Goldi had made from the torn-up letters. Goldi began to throw handfuls into the trash can. Mrs. Howard walked over to Goldi and tightly wrapped her arms around her. Goldi crossed her arms over her chest and made fists, resisting as usual, her mother's hold on her. Mrs. Howard began to squeeze her tightly. Goldi's arms soon fell limp to her sides and closed her eyes as she snuggled her head underneath her mother's chin.

"Your father and I love you very much!" Mrs. Howard whispered, "And the King loves you even more!"

The school day was a nice distraction. No one really spoke to Goldi. All the girls were busy talking about the party. She was fine at lunch just being alone thinking while everything blurred around her. Suddenly, a silhouette appeared on her table.

"Goldi," said a voice.

Goldi looked up.

"Catherine?"

"These are yours. They were the party gifts." Catherine said handing her the rose and the small package.

"Oh," said Goldi, "Thanks."

"This is yours too." Catherine said handing her the necklace.

"Where did you find it?"

"On the terrace stairway. Ariel told me it was you who ran away."

"This used to be my grandmother's. I thought it was lost."

"It's beautiful." Catherine said.

"Thank you."

"Thank you."

"Why are you saying thank you?" Goldi asked surprised.

"Because you gave me my first horse."

"I thought you didn't like my horse. Besides, your parents gave you your first horse." Goldi said with her face down.

"I opened your gift first. How did you know I wanted my own horse?"

"I heard you tell the girls at lunch."

"You were listening?"

"It's what I do at lunch a lot of times. Anyway, it's a **toy** horse."

Catherine smiled. "I named her Goldi."

"You did?"

"Yes, it's just right!"

Goldi smiled.

"Sorry I ran away. I'm just not a real princess."

"Me neither."

"What do you mean?"

"No one in my family has royal blood. My father is rich, but everything else is just a story."

"Oh." Goldi said softly.

Catherine smiled. "There's something else you should know."

"What?"

"My real horse's name is Marigold."

"Really?"

" Yes."

Goldi smiled at Catherine.

"I want to tell you something," said Goldi.

"What?"

"I have a friend. But she's a doll."

"A doll?" asked Catherine surprised.

"Yeah. I talk to her about a lot of things."

"You talk to her?"

"Yes, she listens all the time. I named her Catherine. She IS the name of a real princess"

"Oh!" said Catherine smiling.

"Why are you being nice to me?" Goldi asked.

"Because **you** are nice and giving me that horse was the nicest thing anyone's ever done for me."

"A lot of people are nice to you, Catherine."

"Well, when I sit at the lunch table being nice to everyone, I feel lonely."

"But you are not alone."

"I can be still **feel** alone. Besides, I think you are different."

"Of course, I'm different!"

"I was wondering if you would like to meet Marigold?

"Probably not. Horses are too big." Goldi insisted.

"I know you'll like her."

Even the thought of seeing a horse gave Goldi a shiver of fear.

"I have to think about it," she said.

"She really was nice to me." Goldi told her doll Catherine later that day.

"It was like real friends talking to each other."

Her doll had been sitting in her room so still and quiet for so long. Goldi could tell her anything. She always let Goldi get the words out without interruption. She was just the kind of friend Goldi needed.

"She has the same name as you. Besides you Catherine, I don't really have a friend who is a real person. You are just a doll. I wonder if …. she could be …. a **real** friend?"

Goldi looked at her doll's face closely. She had tried to stop imagining since she figured there was no use in doing so. But at that moment, it was her imagination that seemed to see the biggest smile she had ever seen on her doll's face and a voice inside her whispered: "Yes!"

Catherine's house was almost as big as the Flowers Hotel. A fence surrounding a huge acreage of green. Goldi stood alone by the gate and saw Catherine with Marigold approaching.

"Goldi!" she called.

As they came closer, Goldi clutched her sensory necklace, flapped a little, then breathed.

"Come and pet her." Catherine directed as the gate opened.

Goldi walked slowly closer and gently laid a few fingers on Marigold's neck. Despite a few flicks of her tail, the horse was still.

"Marigold, meet Marigold."

Marigold gave a quick nod.

Goldi belly laughed.

"Want to watch me ride?" asked Catherine.

Goldi nodded.

Catherine mounted and galloped her horse around. Marigold seemed to dance in the green grass like a ballerina.

"Your turn." Catherine said as she finished.

"No! "said Goldi.

"But Marigold has to ride Marigold." Catherine pleaded. "Come on, take a step into this."

Before Goldi could resist, Catherine had placed her foot inside one stirrup.

"No Catherine! I can't!"

"Yes, you can!" Catherine insisted.

Carefully she pushed Goldi's other leg over Marigold and she was soon sitting on Marigold.

"I'm scared!" Goldi cried.

"We'll go slowly." Catherine assured.

"I can't! Please I need to get down!" Goldi cried with tears.

"Marigold is the sweetest horse. You'll see." Catherine said earnestly.

"I don't like this! I can't. Please get me down!" Goldi yelled kicking Marigold a little.

"Goldi! Stop kicking her! She didn't do anything wrong! Just trust me, you'll like this!" Catherine insisted.

Goldi stopped. She had a few left-over tears coming down that she wiped away. She was embarrassed that Catherine had seen the worse in her. But she looked down at Catherine. She was smiling at her. She winked at Goldi and said

"Really, Goldi. You will love it!".

"Okay. "Goldi said sighing. "But just for a little bit."

"Okay!" said Catherine.

Catherine took Marigold by the reins and led her slowly forward.

 Riding on her, she saw a world that she'd never seen when walking on her own two feet. Catherine led Marigold all around. "Good girl!" said Catherine patting Marigold's neck.

Marigold nodded her head and snorted. Both girls laughed. Catherine led Marigold all around the arena. There was sunshine, breeze, and peace.

Mr. Danielson walked over smiling.

"Hello! Would your girls like to go on a carriage ride?" he asked.

"Could we go to our secret place?" Catherine asked.

"Good idea." Mr. Danielson replied.

Danielson

The girls followed Mr. ████████ to the front of a small barn. In front, was a handsome redwood carriage.

"Catherine, are you sure you aren't a real princess?" Goldi asked.

Catherine giggled.

After hitching Marigold to the carriage, Mr. Danielson helped the girls into the carriage and climbed up onto the driver's seat. He made a clicking sound with his mouth and lightly tapped the reins on Marigold. Slowly she trotted out of the fenced area onto a dirt road that led into the woods.

"Where are we going?" asked Goldi as the girls climbed aboard.

"You've got to see this place," replied Marigold.

They hobbled along on a dirt trail surrounded by spring beauty, violets, and green ferns. The carriage stopped in a large clearing where the sunshine brightened up the garden of green. There was a gentle rushing sound of water in the distance.

Before Catherine could lead the way, Goldi immediately ran toward the sound, leaving a shoes and socks trail behind her. Catherine found her stopped on a large rock in the middle of a clear stream. Together the two stood in the water, with their arms spread out, allowing the breeze to comb them with refreshment, and the water ripples to caress their feet.

"Just right!" Catherine said.

"Exactly! said Goldi with her eyes closed and smiling at the sun.

The girls spent much time together taking turns riding Marigold. Goldi learned to love the horse just as much as Catherine did. She loved how Marigold nodded her head when she knew Goldi was aboard. She loved how she gently tip toed when told to slow down. Marigold was absolutely just right to Goldi.

The girls went to the secret place often. There they could talk about anything.

"Catherine," Goldi said with her eyebrows raised "You ARE my friend, right?"

"Of course!" answered Catherine.

"Did you know I have autism?" asked Goldi.

"Well, Mrs. Babcock told us that once when you weren't in the classroom," answered Catherine.

"Do you know what autism is?"

"Not really. Do you?"

"Well, I was born with it and some things bother me but…. actually, I really have no idea!" answered Goldi

"Whatever!" said Catherine.

Goldi giggled and smiled.

"And you're MY friend, right?" Catherine asked in a serious tone.

"Yes, of course!" confirmed Goldi enthusiastically.

"Even though I'm not a real princess?" said Catherine.

"Whatever!" said Goldi giggling. "Someday, maybe we'll both be princesses."

"But you **do** know that's only in fairy tales?" asked Catherine.

"Well, not just in fairy tales," said Goldi rather confidently.

"Well then, only in our dreams!" said Catherine.

Goldi winked at Catherine.

"Some dreams really do come true!" said Goldi smiling.

For some time, the two friends just silently stood there on the river rocks, perfectly content, dreaming with all of their hearts.

Chapter 17 Somebody

2 Corinthians 5:17

Therefore, if anyone is in Christ, he is a new creation, the old has passed away, behold, the new has come.

The week of the Fifth grade Celebration had arrived. The fifth graders thought of themselves more like 6th graders now. No one ever really admitted their fear of being in a new school nor that they felt sorry that they were leaving their childhood. But sometimes a scratch in their voice or a deep sigh, showed they still had to muster up courage to face the fact that they were turning a corner into being a young adult.

"I can't believe in only 7 more days and we will be 6th graders!" said Catherine.

"I know! It's really true!" Goldi said wiggling in her chair.

Suddenly a voice surprised them both.

"May I sit with you?"

There was Ariel.

"You want to sit with us?" asked Catherine.

"Yes, if you'll let me?" Ariel asked with a sheepish smile.

"I guess you can if you want to!" Goldi exclaimed.

"Why do want to sit with us?" asked Catherine suspiciously.

"I'm sorry, Goldiella, I mean Goldi," said Ariel.

"Ariel! You said my name right!" Goldi said.

"Yes, sorry, I've teased you about your name." Said Ariel.

"Okay," said Goldi

"And... sorry that I have made fun of you for believing so much in fairy tales." Ariel explained.

"Well, Ariel, you are right. Fairy tales aren't real." Goldi said.

"I know but I shouldn't have teased you. Anyway, fairy tales aren't so bad. "

"I DO still believe in happily ever after." Goldi said boldly.

"You do?" asked Ariel.

"Sure! "said Goldi smiling. "Just like in the Little Mermaid."

"Yeah, I guess that story did end happily ever after!" said Ariel smiling. "Well, maybe in junior high, maybe...." Ariel stopped short.

"Maybe what?" asked Catherine wondering what Ariel wanted.

"Since we are talking about happily ever after, maybe I could be both of your friends? Ariel asked with eyebrows raised, "That would make me happy."

Catherine looked at Goldi. Goldi looked at Catherine. Both shrugged their shoulders.

"Well, I guess so!" said Goldi smiling.

Ariel's smile was wide and showed her teeth.

Just like that, Ariel "who used to be a mermaid", went from being mean like a stepsister, to being nice like a friend.

'Why do you want to be friends with us anyway?" asked Catherine, "You do know I am not part of royal family like some people think I am, and Goldi is autistic."

"Yes, I'm autistic," said Goldi in a serious tone.

"Well," said Ariel worriedly, she had to think of a good reason to want to be their friend, "Well, I was never a mermaid and maybe none of those things matter."

"Do you really mean that Ariel?" asked Catherine.

"Yes" said Ariel.

"Okay then!" said Catherine.

"It sure will be different in junior high," said Ariel.

"Yeah, "said Catherine. "We will have more than one teacher."

"We will have more homework", added Ariel.

"Whatever!" said Goldi.

The three friends finished their lunch giggling between bites.

The End of the Year Fifth Grade Celebration brought a crowd of people unlike the student body had ever seen. Families and students of the fifth-grade class gathered in the school auditorium. Mrs. Babcock began the assembly with a speech:

"In many ways, the last year of elementary school is like a long walk, in the woods. If you go on a long walk, you must plan. You have to wear good walking shoes. You should take a snack and some water. You might take some rain gear. A compass helps you find your way. There is a story of a girl who went into the woods skipping along enjoying herself. There were flowers, trees, and birds singing so sweetly. But there was also a house deep in the woods, and in that house lived a family of bears! Goldilocks walked right in without fear. She tried the porridge, sat on the chairs, and slept on the beds. I'm sure when Goldilocks got home, she had learned a lot. But all along she was very brave, and she took risks. She had real determination. On our journey this year, the fifth graders have had to try all kinds of things. Sometimes the work they did was really hard, sometimes they found it very easy. Sometimes they found the work was just right. But no matter what, they tried their best and learned that just by trying, they became better someones than before. It has been a long walk in the woods, but I am pleased to say that they are now ready for Junior High. We wish them well as they continue their adventure!"

Everyone applauded. Mrs. Babcock began calling names alphabetically to receive their graduation certificate: Ariel Anderson, walked up straight and tall like she was already in junior high. Maria Griggs appeared to shake a little. Catherine Danielson gracefully waved to her parents. Marigold Ellanora Howard jumped and flapped across the stage, repeatedly when handed her certificate. Then they were all standing shoulder to shoulder in a line that spanned the whole length of the stage. Each held their graduation certificates beaming as the class photo was taken.

"We invite you all to take a look at the student displays. They all tell about some special somebodies in our fifth grade. Please enjoy our "Me Museum" announced Mrs. Babcock.

Parents and guest viewed the displays showing a lot of Somebodies. There were trophies, soccer jerseys, medals, artwork, and photos of kids missing teeth and kids blowing out candles on their birthday cakes. Each student had written their thoughts about their treasures and the somebody that they had grown to become.

Catherine's display had the china horse that Goldi given her, a picture of the ocean, a piggy bank, and a river rock. She wrote *I am somebody from a rich family. I have seen horses run wild along the ocean shore and my house is as almost as big as the Flowers Hotel. I am somebody who owns a real horse. I named her after a true friend. People think I am somebody who is a real princess. I am really not. But when my friend and I go to our secret place and stand on the river rocks with the ripples washing our feet, my friend tells me someday we really will be princesses. When we are there together, and she tells me this, I get a happily ever after feeling. Thanks to my friend, I am starting to believe that maybe someday I really will be a princess. I am Catherine Elizabeth Danielson.*

Goldi's table display had two storybooks of Cinderella and Goldilocks, her grandmother's necklace, and a pot of marigolds. Goldi wrote in large print: *I am somebody named after a flower that blooms a long time. I am somebody with a doll that I named Catherine after a real princess. I am somebody with the middle name of my grandmother. I am somebody like Goldilocks because I like everything just right. I am somebody with autism. I jump and flap and pace when things **aren't** just right. Some people say I need to grow up. Well, I **am** growing up. I am smiling, laughing, and being brave. But mostly, I'm dreaming. I'm dreaming about someday when I won't have autism. I won't have to dream about being a real princess. I will BE a real princess. More than that, I will be a perfect princess who will live happily ever after. I believe with all of my heart that this will come true. I am Marigold Ellanora Howard.*

Made in the USA
Lexington, KY
17 June 2019